Joe on the Go

PEGGY PERRY ANDERSON

sandpiper

Green Light Readers

Houghton Mifflin Harcourt

Boston New York

The Library of Congress has cataloged the hardcover edition as follows:
Anderson, Peggy Perry.
Joe on the go/Peggy Perry Anderson.
p. cm.
Summary: Joe the frog wants to be on the go, but even at a family reunion,
he is out of luck, as everyone says they are too busy, or he is too fast, too slow, too big,
or too small to go with them, until Grandma invites him to go with her on a special outing.
[1. Family reunions—Fiction. 2. Play—Fiction. 3. Frogs—Fiction. 4. Stories in rhyme.]
I. Title.
PZ8.3.A5484Joe 2007
[E]—dc22

ISBN: 978-0-618-77331-2 hardcover
ISBN: 978-0-547-74563-3 paperback

Manufactured in China
LEO 10 9 8 7 6 5 4 3 2 1

4500355925

"Let's go!" said Joe to Mother dear.
"Sorry, Joe, I am busy here."

"Let's go!" said Joe. Dad said, "No way.
Today is family meeting day."

Then came cousins, uncles, and aunts.
They came to visit, eat, and dance.

"Let's go! Let's go!" said Joe with a cheer.

"That's silly," they said.
"We just got here."

"Let's go!" said Joe to Uncle Fred,
who had to talk to Merle instead.

"Let's go!" said Joe to Uncle Drew.
"I'm cooking," Drew said. "Ask Auntie Lou."

"Let's go!" said Joe to Auntie Lou.
"Honey, I'm too slow for you."

"Let's go!" said Joe to Uncle Bull.
"Later, Joe. I'm not quite full."

"Hold real still," said Grandpa Proud.

"Let's go!" said Joe to the posing crowd.

"Let's go!" said Joe
to Baby Sprout.
But her mother came
and took her out.

"Let's go!" said Joe to Cousin Matt.
"Joe, you are too big for that!"

"This is just the size for you.
Move along on your big choo-choo!"

"Let's go!" said Joe. Cousin Jeff said, "No!"

"Joe, skateboards are not for you.
Roller skating would be safer, too."

"Please wait for me," cried Joe.
But the skaters said, "You are too slow."

"Let's go!"
yelled Joe
to Pete
and Paul.

"No," they said, "you are too small."

"Let's go!" cried Joe to Cousin Trent,
who grabbed the bike and away he went.

"No," said Joe, "that's not what I meant!"

Then he sat down and began to bawl.
"Too fast, too slow, too big, too small.
No one will go with me at all!"

"Come on, Joe. Let's go!"

"Oh, boy," said Joe. "Can it be true?
Grandma, is that
really you?"